Can I Have a TYRANNOSAURUS REX, Dad? Can I? Please!?

by Lois G. Grambling
Pictures by Penny L. C. Hauffe

Troll
BridgeWater Books

Can I have a
Tyrannosaurus rex, Dad?
Can I?
PLEASE!?
If I had a Tyrannosaurus rex, Dad . . .

When we went to the mall
during Mall Madness Week
my Tyrannosaurus rex could go with us.
And when we got there
he'd search for a parking space.
And when he found one
he'd point to it.
And you'd get it.
Quick!
And no other driver would try to beat you to it.
Like they do now.

Not with my
Tyrannosaurus rex
glaring down at them!

Can I have a Tyrannosaurus rex, Dad?
Can I?
PLEASE!?
If I had a Tyrannosaurus rex, Dad . . .
Grandma wouldn't have to call
the volunteer fire department
every time Tabitha got chased up the apple tree
by that mean dog
Wolfgang.
'Cause my Tyrannosaurus rex could just reach up
and pluck Tabitha out safely.
And hand her down to Grandma.

And then maybe teach that
Wolfgang a lesson.
One he'd never EVER forget.

Can I have a Tyrannosaurus rex, Dad?
Can I?
PLEASE!?
If I had a Tyrannosaurus rex, Dad . . .
I'd invite him to my birthday party.
And then you wouldn't have to
take us to the movies.
Or bowling.

'Cause we could climb up on my Tyrannosaurus rex
and he'd gallop with us.
Fast!
Around and around the backyard.
And the ground
would roll
and rumble.
And we'd all be screaming and screeching
and having a wonderful time!

And my birthday party would be the best party ever!

Can I have a Tyrannosaurus rex, Dad?
Can I?
PLEASE!?

If I had a Tyrannosaurus rex, Dad . . .
He'd be great for show–and–tell.
Much better than
Clarissa's ant farm that she brings in
every year.
Or Adam's collection of shark teeth his grandfather
just gave him.

And if my teacher
said my Tyrannosaurus rex had to leave
right after show–and–tell,
he could spend the rest of the day
in the principal's office.
Mr. Grumble wouldn't mind!

Can I have a Tyrannosaurus rex, Dad?
Can I?
PLEASE!?

If I had a Tyrannosaurus rex, Dad . . .
When Roy asked me to spend the night with him
in a tent
in his backyard,
I'd take my Tyrannosaurus rex with me.
And then I wouldn't have to worry
about all those wolves and bears and coyotes
circling around out there in the dark
trying to get in and eat me up!
'Cause my Tyrannosaurus rex would be
out there in the dark
protecting me.

Can I have a Tyrannosaurus rex, Dad?
Can I?
PLEASE!?
If I had a Tyrannosaurus rex, Dad . . .
When we go to the beach this summer
my Tyrannosaurus rex could go with us.

And we wouldn't have to take along
our big beach umbrella
like we do now
to keep the hot sun off us.
'Cause my Tyrannosaurus rex would.
And we could stretch out in the sand.
And nobody would even think of running past us
and kicking sand on us.
Not even accidentally!

Can I have a Tyrannosaurus rex, Dad?
Can I?
PLEASE!?
If I had a Tyrannosaurus rex, Dad . . .
We could put a sign in
our front yard that said

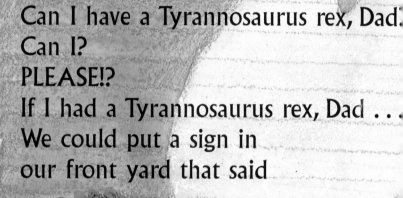

This property
protected by
a very hungry
T-rex

And with the sign in our front yard
we wouldn't have to worry
about burglars breaking into our house.

'Cause no burglars—
not even really dumb ones—
would break into a house and rob it
when it was protected by
a very hungry Tyrannosaurus rex!

Can I have a Tyrannosaurus rex, Dad?
Can I?
PLEASE!?
If I had a Tyrannosaurus rex, Dad . . .
He could be one of the forwards
on our soccer team.
And after we got him a uniform
(E-X-T-R-A L-A-R-G-E, of course)
he'd look great!
And score lots of goals.
And we'd win every game!

So . . .
Can I have a Tyrannosaurus rex, Dad?
Can I?
PLEASE!?

No?????

Okay
then
if I can't have a Tyrannosaurus rex, Dad . . .
Can I maybe have a bird instead?
Can I?
PLEASE!?
Like maybe a parrot?
Or an ostrich?
'Cause last week I bought this really
neat looking egg
at a garage sale.
And I've been keeping it warm
in my room
ever since.

And . . .
Hey! Wait a sec, Dad.
Do you hear some loud
flapping?

Oh!
WOW!
AWESOME!

Can I have a pterodactyl, Dad?
Can I?
PLEASE!?
If I had a pterodactyl, Dad . . .

To all the Gramblings, who have enriched
and brought so much joy to my life.
— L. G.

To my family—you give me wings
so that I may fly.
— P. L. C. H.

Text copyright © 2000 by Lois G. Grambling.
Illustrations copyright © 2000 by Penny L. C. Hauffe and H. B. Lewis.

Published by BridgeWater Books, an imprint and registered trademark
of Troll Communications L.L.C.

Printed in the United States of America.

10   9   8   7   6   5   4   3   2

LIBRARY OF CONGRESS CATALOGING-IN-PUBLICATION DATA
Grambling, Lois G.
Can I have a Tyrannosaurus rex, Dad? Can I? Please!? / by Lois G. Grambling;
pictures by Penny L. C. Hauffe.
p.   cm.
Summary: A boy comes up with many creative reasons why a Tyrannosaurus rex
would be a good and helpful pet to have.
ISBN 0-8167-4946-9
[I. Tyrannosaurus rex—Fiction. 2. Dinosaurs—Fiction. 3. Fathers and sons—Fiction.]
I. Hauffe, Penny L. C., ill. II. Title.
PZ7.G7655Cand   1999
[E]—dc21   98-21300